S0-CGS-497

## Mel Bay Presents

# CONCEPTS FOR THE CLASSICAL AND JAZZ GUITAR

### by Jimmy Wyble & Ron Berman

---

## CD CONTENTS
### (program numbers correspond to book CD numbers)

| | | | | | | | |
|---|---|---|---|---|---|---|---|
| 1 | CD #1 [:24] | 15 | CD #15 [:23] | 29 | CD #29 [:25] | 43 | CD #43 [:19] |
| 2 | CD #2 [:21] | 16 | CD #16 [:22] | 30 | CD #30 [:23] | 44 | CD #44 [:20] |
| 3 | CD #3 [:22] | 17 | CD #17 [:17] | 31 | CD #31 [:19] | 45 | CD #45 [:33] |
| 4 | CD #4 [:24] | 18 | CD #18 [:22] | 32 | CD #32 [:30] | 46 | CD #46 [:33] |
| 5 | CD #5 [:21] | 19 | CD #19 [:21] | 33 | CD #33 [:21] | 47 | CD #47 [1:28] |
| 6 | CD #6 [:22] | 20 | CD #20 [:20] | 34 | CD #34 [:21] | 48 | CD #48 [3:45] |
| 7 | CD #7 [:21] | 21 | CD #21 [:22] | 35 | CD #35 [:21] | 49 | CD #49 [:57] |
| 8 | CD #8 [:23] | 22 | CD #22 [:19] | 36 | CD #36 [:35] | 50 | CD #50 [1:00] |
| 9 | CD #9 [:23] | 23 | CD #23 [:22] | 37 | CD #37 [:23] | 51 | CD #51 [:30] |
| 10 | CD #10 [:26] | 24 | CD #24 [:24] | 38 | CD #38 [:20] | 52 | CD #52 [:21] |
| 11 | CD #11 [:27] | 25 | CD #25 [:21] | 39 | CD #39 [:28] | 53 | CD #53 [:21] |
| 12 | CD #12 [:23] | 26 | CD #26 [:24] | 40 | CD #40 [:23] | 54 | CD #54 [:57] |
| 13 | CD #13 [:21] | 27 | CD #27 [:20] | 41 | CD #41 [:34] | 55 | CD #55 [:23] |
| 14 | CD #14 [:20] | 28 | CD #28 [26] | 42 | CD #42 [:19] | 56 | CD #56 [:35] |

© 2000 BY MEL BAY PUBLICATIONS, INC., PACIFIC, MO 63069.

*Visit us on the Web at www.melbay.com — E-mail us at email@melbay.com*

I would like to pay homage to John Collins, a guitarist of supreme taste and great harmonic beauty. His life is the history of jazz guitar…and to Russell Malone, of the young generation, whose spirit is the embodiment of all that has come before him, a complete jazz guitarist.

Sincerely,

*Jimmy Wyble*

Jimmy Wyble

---

Dear Jimmy,

It's been a long time since we've talked. I've been working and writing and doing pretty well. I hope that you are doing well too!

I finally completed the first part of your 20 exercises for guitar that you so kindly gave to me through Sid. I had fun working out some permutations from your notes.

The mathematics of permutations is fun. When you multiply 1 times 2 times 3 times 4 times 5 times 6, etc., the combinations quickly reach staggering proportions.

I like to mention to students that there are 6 combinations of triads. Four note chords/arpeggios produce 24 combinations. Pentatonics have 120 permutations within an octave and whole tone scales produce 720 possiblities. Then it really gets out there as you reach the 7 through 12 notes of our equal tempered tonal systems.

Any seven note scale has 5040 different ways of being played within one octave without repetition. When I see some student tearing away at major scales ascending or decending diatonically, I feel like telling them "Hey, that's great but what about the other 5038 ways of playing the same scale?"

Then I casually mention that our diminished or octatonic scales produce 40,320 ways.

Nine note scales have 362,880 permutations.

Ten note scales have 3,628,800 permutations.

An eleven note scale would have 39,916,800 permutations.

Finally our 12-tone system produces 479,001,600 permutations.

It is one of the greatest joys in the universe to be able to experience music filled with so many variations of chords, melodies, harmonies, and rhythms that so many musicians have done, are presently doing, and will continue to do long after we're gone.

Best wishes to you and Lily,

*Ron Berman*

Ron Berman

# Introduction

Working through the material in this book will stretch your ears and fingers, broaden your harmonic palette and strengthen music reading skills. Although written for guitarists, this book is filled with pages of music that can be adapted for use by any instrument or ensemble.

Take any example or fragment and learn to play it. Use any idea that appeals to you and try to fit it into something that you feel comfortable with. Try to insert it into an arrangement or improvisation. All of the material including melodic lines and permutations can be split up for use with one or more instruments playing the individual lines. Ensembles can take chord voicings and assign notes to each member to generate different harmonic textures.

One of the purposes of this book is to illustrate that any musical idea may be used for improvisation, permutation, composition, reharmonization or counterpoint. The goal is to get these concepts and techniques into your ears and fingers and apply them while having some musical fun communicating, creating and exploring the musical universe. Don't be discouraged if your early attempts don't work out. It takes time to develop these skills, but they are worth it.


Sincerely,

Jimmy and Ron

# Jimmy Wyble's 20 Exercises For Guitar

**CD#1**

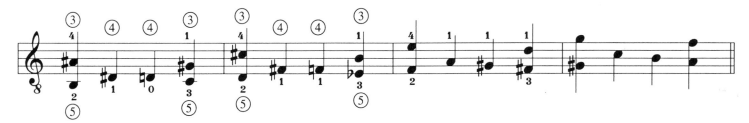

**CD#1**   Permutation of #1 beats: 3-4-2-1

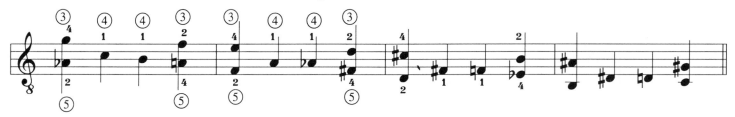

**CD#2**   Permutation of #1 descending

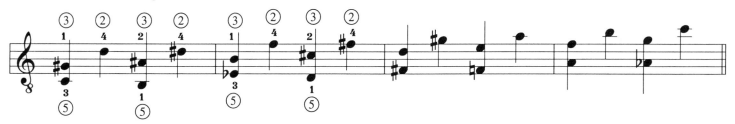

**CD#2**   #1 Passing tone 8va

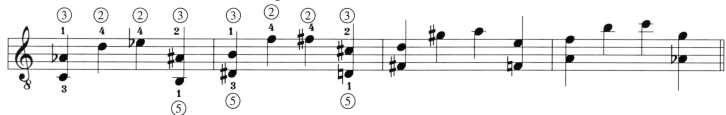

**CD#3**   Permutation of #1 Passing tone 8va

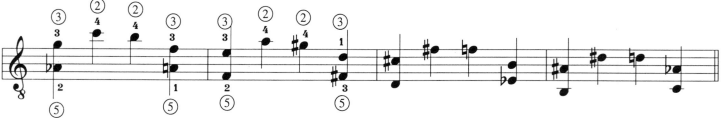

**CD#3**   Permutation of #1 Passing tone 8va

**CD#4** Pattern: Major Seventh to minor sixth
top voice down M2-up P4 bottom voice up m2- up M2

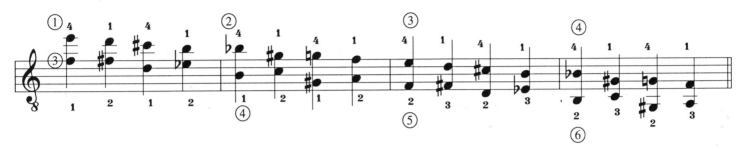

**CD#4** Pattern: Major Seventh to minor sixth
top voice down M2-down m2 bottom voice up m2- down M3

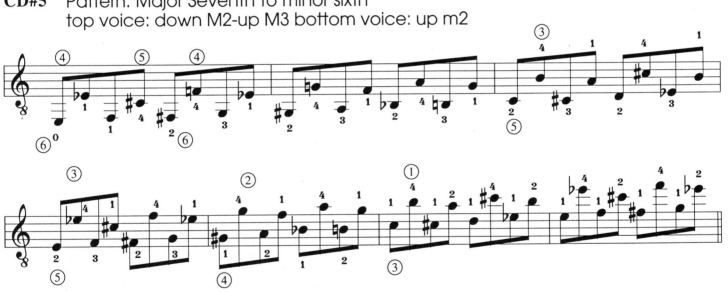

**CD#5** Pattern: Major Seventh to minor sixth
top voice: down M2-up M3 bottom voice: up m2

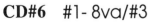

**CD#6** #1- 8va/#3

**CD#6**   #2

**CD#7**   #2 Retrograde

**CD#7**   Combination of #1 and #2

**CD#8**   Combination of #1 and #2

**CD#8**   Combination of #1 and #2

**CD#9**   Combination of #1 and #2

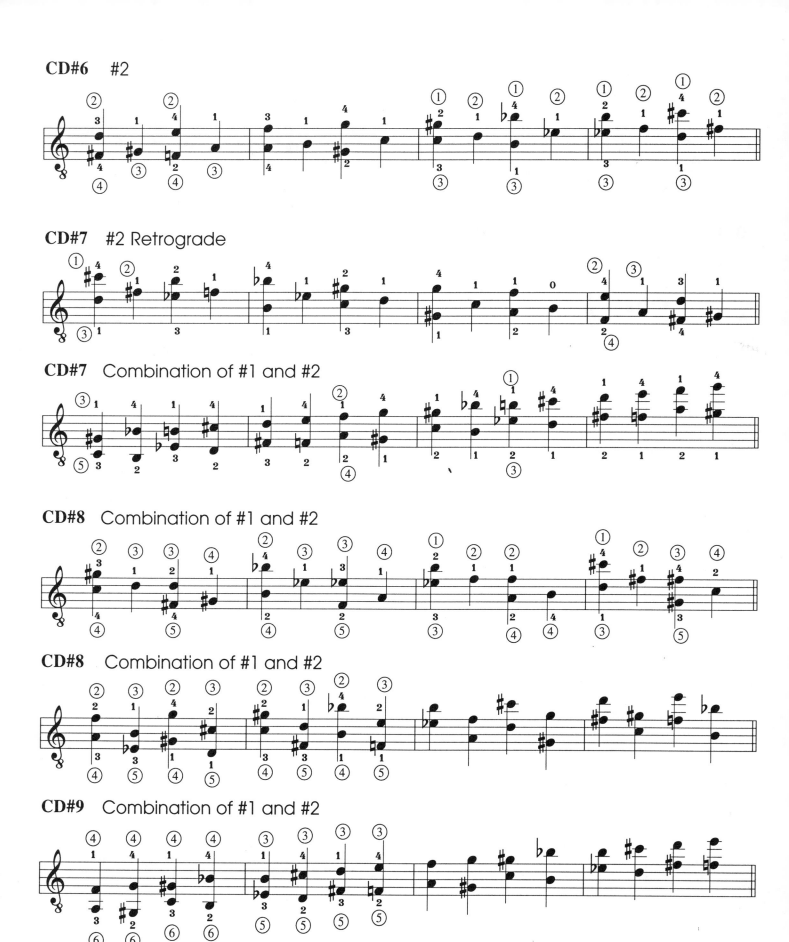

CD#14   #5 Permutation

CD#14

CD#15

#5 Permutation

CD#15

#5 Permutation

CD#16   #6

CD#16   #6 Permutation

CD#17   #6 Permutation

CD#17   #6 Permutation

8

**CD#18** #6 Permutation

**CD#18** #6 Permutation

**CD#19** #6 Permutation

**CD#19**

#6 Permutation

Sequence: 7    2    3    8    5    6    1    4

**CD#20** 2-Note groups from #6 with inverted notes in 2nd and 4th pairings

**CD#20** #7-Same as #6

**CD#21** #8-Pattern 1-Ascending

**CD#21** #8-Pattern 1-Descending

**CD#22**   #8-Pattern 2-Ascending

**CD#22**   #8-Pattern 2-Descending

**CD#23**   Permutation #8

**CD#23**   Permutation #8

**CD#24**

Combining both note choices of #8 into triplets

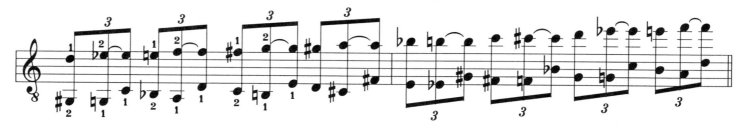

**CD#24**

**CD#25** Triplet Permutation of #8

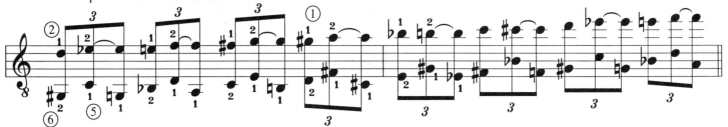

**CD#25** Triplet Permutation of #8

**CD#26**

Triplet Permutation of #8

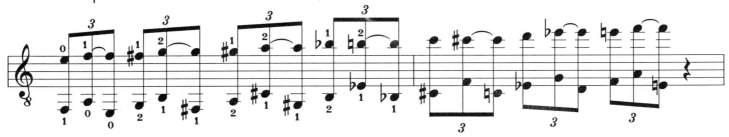

**CD#26** Triplet Permutation of #8

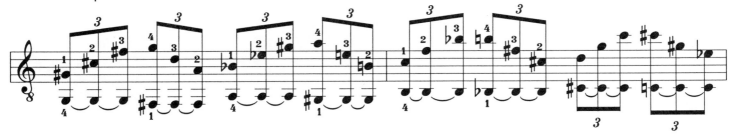

**CD#27** Triplet Permutation of #8

**CD#27**

Triplet Permutation of #8

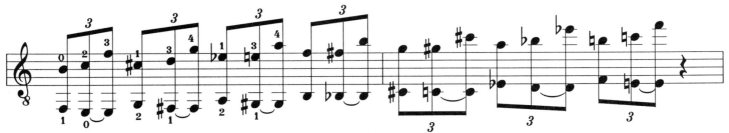

**CD#28** #9-Sets of 3 placed in Triplets

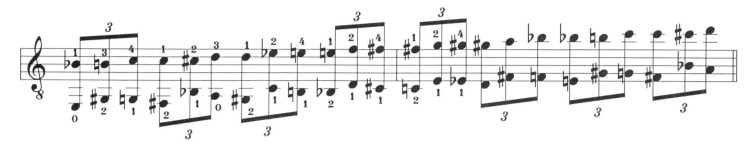

**CD#28** Triplet Permutation of #9

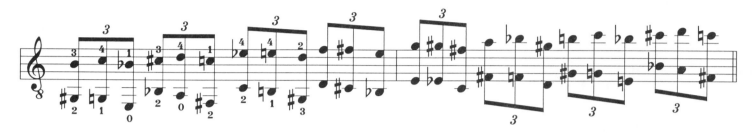

**CD#29** Triplet Permutation of #9

**CD#29** #10

**CD#30** #10 Descending

**CD#30** #10 Permutation Ascending

**CD#31** #10 Permutation Descending

**CD#31** #10 Permutation Ascending

**CD#32** #10 Permutation Descending

**CD#32** #11 (Sustain Whole Notes Where Possible)

**CD#33** #11 Permutation

**CD#34**

#11 Permutation (Drop last note for 5-note figure)

**CD#35**

#11 Permutation (Drop last note for 5-note figure)

14

**CD#36** #11 Permutation (Drop last note for 5-note figure)

**CD#36** #11 Permutation (Drop last note for 5-note figure)

**CD#37**

#11 Permutation (Drop last note for 5-note figure)

**CD#38** #11 Permutation (Drop last note for 5-note figure)

The four-note voicings on this page are derived from exercise eleven. 120 (four-note) voicings can be derived from the five-note pattern below. The five examples below permutated through the scale is a mere fraction of what is to be found there.

Voicing derived from top four notes: 2-3-4-5 in exercise 11
**CD#39**       then carried through the entire scale.

**CD#39** Voicing from notes: 1-3-4-5

**CD#40** Voicing from notes: 1-2-4-5

**CD#40** Voicing from notes: 1-2-3-4

**CD#41** Voicing from notes: 1-2-3-5

# Jimmy Wyble's Ex. #11 Converted Into "Harmonic Minor"

**CD#41** #11 (Sustain Whole Notes)

**CD#42** #11 Permutation

**CD#43**

#11 Permutation (Drop last note for 5-note figure)

**CD#44** #11 Permutation (Drop last note for 5-note figure)

Voicing derived from top four notes: 2-3-4-5 in
exercise 11 then carried through the entire scale.

**CD#47**

**CD#47** Voicing from notes: 1-3-4-5

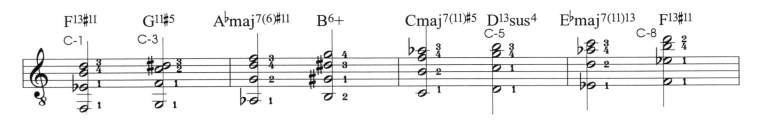

**CD#47** Voicing from notes: 1-2-4-5

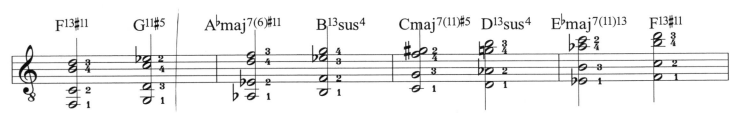

**CD#47** Voicing from notes: 1-2-3-4

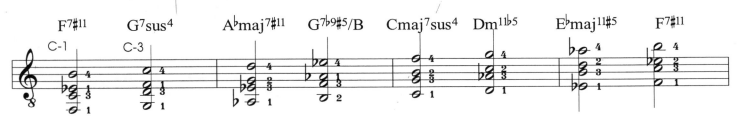

**CD#47** Voicing from notes: 1-2-3-5

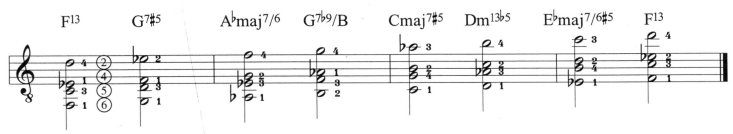

# Jimmy Wyble's Ex. #11 Converted Into "Jazz Melodic Minor"

**CD#48** #11 (Sustain Whole Notes Where Possible)

**CD#48** #11 Permutation

**CD#48**

#11 Permutation (Drop last note for 5-note figure)

**CD#48** #11 Permutation (Drop last note for 5-note figure)

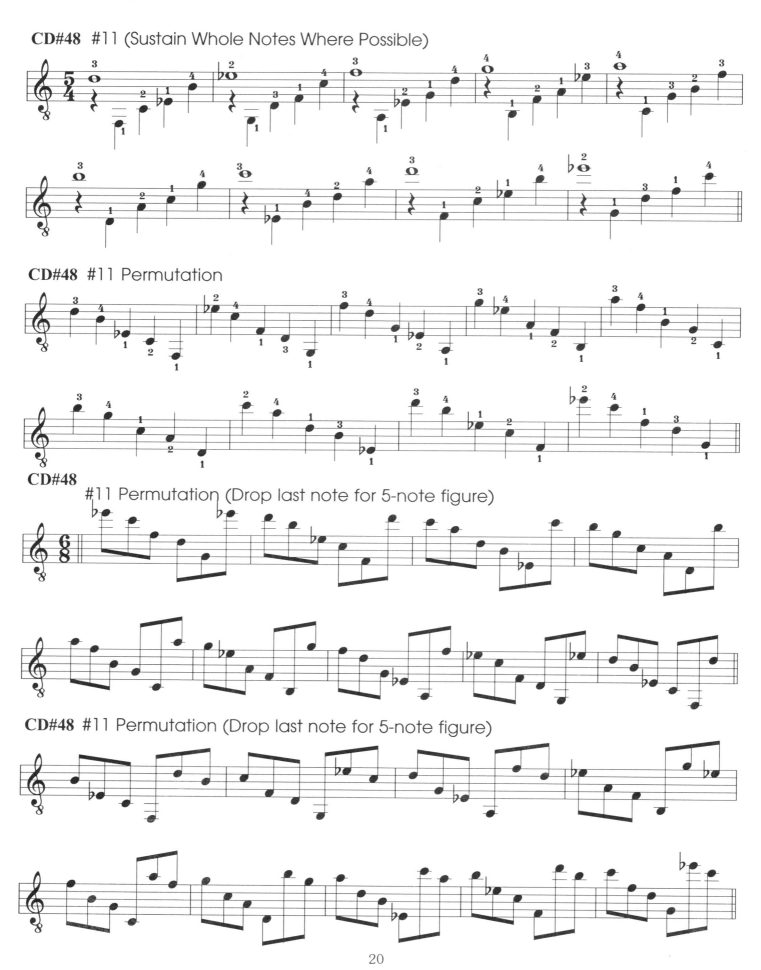

CD#48 #11 Permutation (Drop last note for 5-note figure)

CD#48 #11 Permutation (Drop last note for 5-note figure)

CD#48 #11 Permutation (Drop last note for 5-note figure)

1   2   3   4   5

Voicing derived from top four notes: 2-3-4-5 in exercise 11
then carried through the entire scale.

**CD#48**

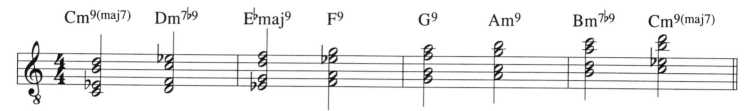

**CD#48** Voicing from notes: 1-3-4-5

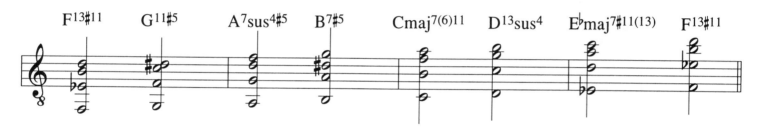

**CD#48** Voicing from notes: 1-2-4-5

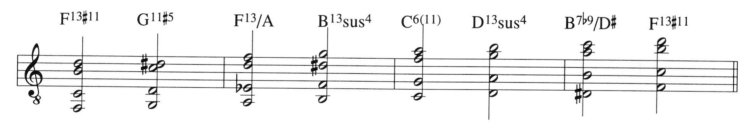

**CD#48** Voicing from notes: 1-2-3-4

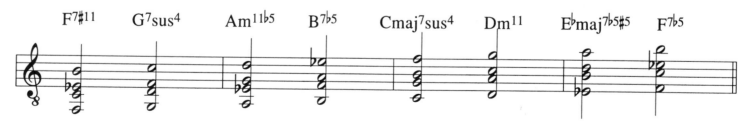

**CD#48** Voicing from notes: 1-2-3-5

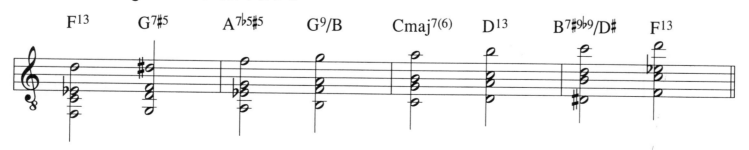

**CD#49** #12

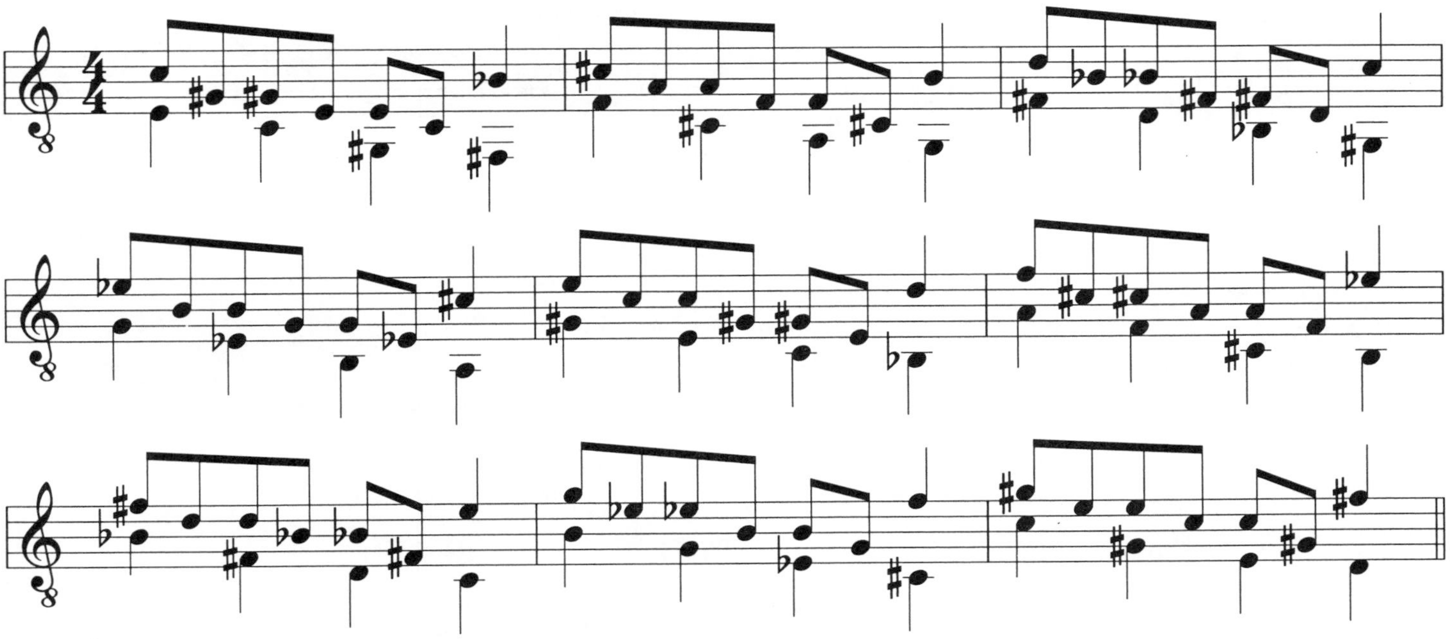

**CD#49** #12 Permutation

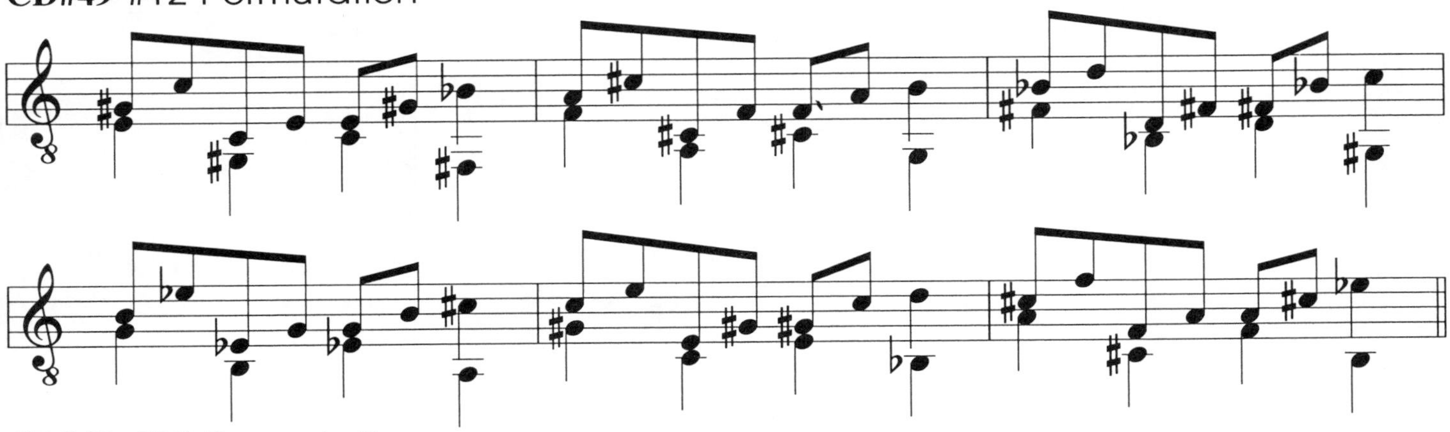

**CD#49** #12 Permutation

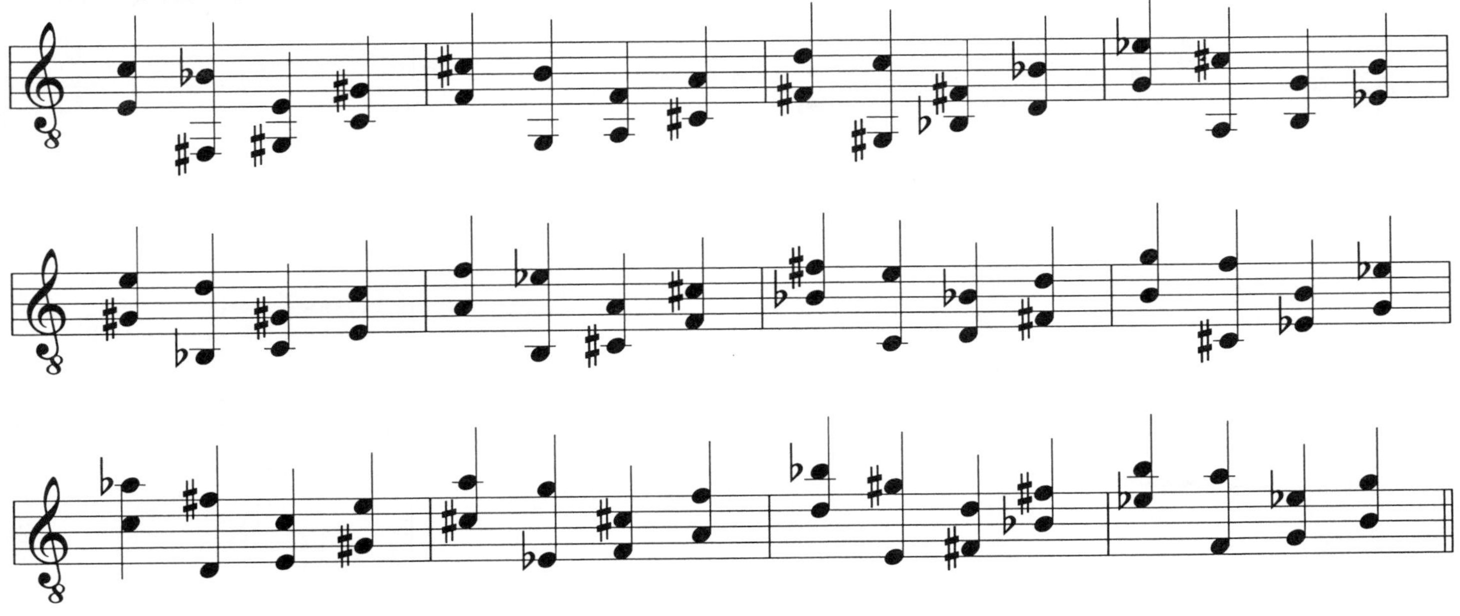

**CD#50** #13 (#12 played up a major third)

**CD#50** #13 Permutation

**CD#50**  #13 Fragments

**CD#50** #13 Fragments

**CD#53** Ex. #16

**CD#53** Permutation of Ex. #16

**CD#53** Permutation of Ex. #16

**CD#54** Ex. #17

**CD#54** Ex. #17-Retrograde

**CD#54** Ex. #18

**CD#54** Permutation of Ex. #18

**CD#54** Permutation of Ex. #18

**CD#55** Ex. #19

**CD#55** Permutation of Ex. #19

**CD#56** Ex. #20

**CD#56** Permutation of Ex. #20

*Ron Berman*

*Jimmy Wyble*

**Ron Berman** received a Masters Degree in Composition from the New England Conservatory in 1978. He studied jazz guitar with Mick Goodrick and Chuck Wayne, composition with George Russell and arranging and orchestration with Jaki Byard and Phil Wilson. Ron resided in Paris for two years, then moved to Los Angeles in 1981. The finger-style guitarist attributes his evolution to all the wonderful musicians he has associated with, especially Astrid, his lovely wife, pianist and sight-reading partner. Ron also treasures his friendship with Kenton Youngstrom, Sid Jacobs, Joe Diorio, Jimmy Wyble and Jeff Gardner. They are delightful sources of inspiration. He plays a Rodger Borys 1986 B120 and uses Thomastik-Infeld flatwound strings.

**Jimmy Wyble** recorded with western swing bands led by Bob Wills and Spade Cooley, and played with the Sons of the Pioneers, Gene Autry, Lena Horne, Steve Lawrence and Eydie Gorme. His TV credits include: The Kraft Music Hall Specials, Phyllis Diller Show, Don Rickles and Andy Williams Shows and specials by Bing Crosby, Flip Wilson and Dick Clark. He spent nine years with Red Norvo's group, as well as filling the guitar chair in Benny Goodman's band and Frank Sinatra's traveling rhythm section. A studio guitarist from 1967 to 1983, Jimmy was a member of the famous *"five Guitar"* group led by Tony Rizzi. His main guitar is a Roger Borys B120 that he has used since 1983.

# THE JIMMY WYBLE SPECIAL

**BODY**

Carved spruce top
Laminated flamed maple back
16" wide at lower bout
19" long
2 $^3/_4$" deep

**NECK**

1 $^3/_4$" wide at nut
25.1" scale length
Ebony fingerboard
Flamed maple neck

Suspended Armstrong pickup
Ebony bridge and pickguard
Sunburst, blonde, or amber finish
Total weight 6 pounds

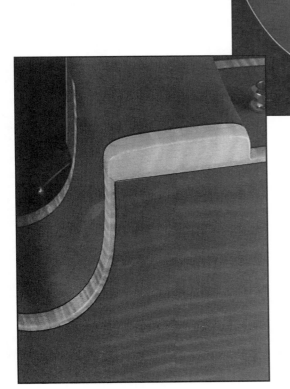

## THE JIMMY WYBLE SPECIAL

The first one was made for Jimmy Wyble for the comfortable body size. The carved spruce top with suspended pickup makes a clean powerful response.

BORYS INSTRUMENTS • 58 Shelburne Shopping Park • Shelburne, Vermont 05482 • (802) 985-1461